Carly's Island Advent

March of the Sea Turtles

Joanne Simon Tailele

Illustrated by Joe Eckstein

Naples, Florida

*Special thanks for the love and support of
Marco Island Writers Inc. for their encouragement
in all my writing endeavors.*

*Also special thanks to the brilliant illustrator, Joe Eckstein,
who has brought Carly and Ranger Todd to life.*

Text copyright © 2022 Joanne Simon Tailele
Illustration copyright © 2022 Joe Eckstein

All rights reserved. No part of this may be reproduced, transmitted or stored in an information retrieval system in any form or by any means. Graphic, electronic, or mechanical, including photocopy, taping, and recording, without prior written permission from the publisher.

This is a work of fiction. Names, characters and incidents are either the products of the author's or artist's imagination.

Published by Simon Publishing LLC

Cover & Interior Design by Imagine!® Studios
www.ArtsImagine.com

ISBN: 978-1-7361881-8-7 (soft cover)
ISBN: 978-1-7361881-9-4 (hard cover)
ISBN: 978-0-578235899 (ebook)

Library of Congress Control Number: 2022901891

First Printing: April 2022

This book is dedicated to my granddaughter,

Cooper Rae Space

Can you help Carly find the little run-away turtle?
He has jumped on to every two-page spread
and he needs your help to find them all!

In the next Carly's Island Adventure, you may
need to find a dolphin, or an eagle or an owl.
They will be hiding in every book.

Ring ring. Carly's alarm clock went off when it was still dark outside.

"Is it time to see the turtles now?" Carly said as she stretched and rubbed the sleep from her eyes.

"Almost," said her mommy.

Carly was excited to go with her neighbor, Ranger Todd. He was taking her to learn about the loggerhead turtles on the beaches of Marco Island.

She dressed herself in her favorite red overalls and blue striped shirt. Mommy braided her hair and made them chocolate chip pancakes with real maple syrup for breakfast.

Ding Dong. Carly ran to the front door and waited for Mommy to open it.

"Good morning, Carly. Good morning, Mrs. Jones," said Ranger Todd.

"Good morning, Ranger Todd, can we go to see the turtles now?" Carly asked excitedly.

Yes, Carly. It's time. You'd better put your sandals on."

Carly looked down at her bare feet and wiggled her toes. "Oh, I forgot." She giggled.

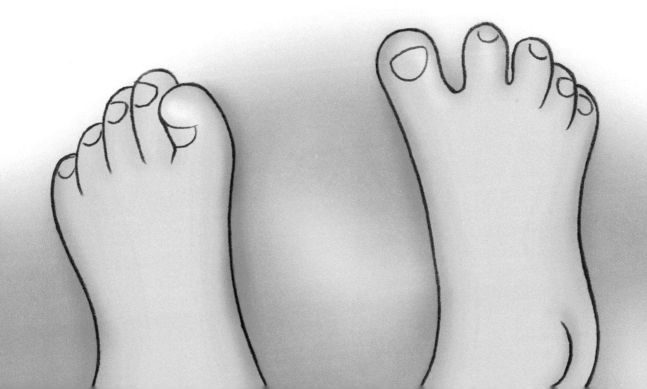

"I'm ready now." She smiled and took Ranger Todd's hand.

"Have fun, Carly," said Mommy. "Stay with Ranger Todd and listen to what he says."

"I will." Carly skipped along and climbed up into his big truck. "Why do we have to go out in the dark to see the turtles, Ranger Todd?"

He buckled her into her seat explaining, "The mother turtles lay their eggs and bury them in the sand. We roped off the nest with tape so no one would step on the nest and break the eggs. When the babies are ready to hatch, they follow the moon into the ocean where they will grow up.

"I can't wait to see them. Can I pick them up . . . or keep one?"

Ranger Todd frowned. "Oh no, Carly. You must not touch them. They must get to the ocean all by themselves. They are wild and need to stay wild.

The moonlight lit up the beach and made the sand look pure white. "Sit down here," Ranger Todd said very quietly. He pointed to a spot on the sand beside the yellow tape.

"Is the Mommy turtle in the nest with the eggs?" whispered Carly.

Ranger Todd shook his head. "No, she's already out in the sea. The babies have to do this all by themselves."

They waited and waited. Carly watched the sand inside the yellow tape. She didn't see anything move. "When are they coming?" Carly was getting tired of waiting.

"When they are ready," said Ranger Todd. "You can't rush Mother Nature."

DO NOT DISTURB
SEA TURTLE
NEST

Carly smiled. "I know what that means. Daddy said that Mother Nature is not a real person, like my mommy, but she is what makes all the flowers bloom and animals be born."

Finally, Carly saw the sand inside the tape move. "Look," she said, pointing.

"They're digging their way out."

First one little turtle, not much bigger than a
shiny new quarter, crawled out of the sand.

Then another, and another.
Pretty soon there were 10, then 20,
and then more than Carly could count.
They crawled out of the sand and
slowly pushed their way
toward the water.

They left tiny little trails in the sand. Carly watched them crawl across the smooth sand.

They reached a sandcastle in the sand. They tried to climb over it, but they were too little. One fell backwards onto his back.

"We are going to have to help him." Ranger Todd gently lifted the tiny turtle and placed it back on his legs.

"Carly, can you help the turtles get to the sea?"

Carly's eyes lit up. "How can I help?

"Go around to the other side and knock down the castle and smooth out the sand. That way they can crawl into the ocean. Be very careful not to scoop up any turtles."

Carly pushed over the sandcastle and carefully flattened out the sand with her hands.

The first baby turtle crawled over the smooth sand and into the water. Then the next followed, and the next.

The sun was coming up on the other side of the island when the last one disappeared into the dark water. Ranger Todd stood and brushed the sand from his pants.

"Good job, Carly. What did you learn today?"

Carly jumped up and brushed the sand off her knees. "When we are done making sandcastles, we should always knock them down and make the sand smooth for the turtles."

Ranger Todd nodded. "That's right. Especially in the spring when the eggs are hatching."

"Will the turtles ever come back here?" asked Carly.

"Some of them. They'll come back to this beach to lay their own eggs, when they are grown-up mommy turtles."

"Thanks Ranger Todd. What great adventure can we see next time?"

About the Author

Joanne Simon Tailele grew up in the Youngstown, Ohio area, and wrote her first short story at the age of ten. Beginning her commercial writing career in 2010, it took multiple publications before she realized that her brand is mother-daughter stories. As a mother of four, a grandmother of ten, and a great-grandmother of one, family is a natural topic. Ms. Tailele has published three women's fiction novels, two biographies, and two children's books. She is currently adding to her children's book series, *Carly's Island Adventures*. Ms. Tailele is also the owner of Simon Publishing LLC (**www.SimonPublishingLLC.com**), a small independent press catering to the authors that seek a personal touch. When not writing, editing, or publishing, she dabbles in real estate. She loves spending time on the beaches of the Gulf of Mexico and lives in Naples, Florida, with her beloved husband and two ornery cats. You can learn more about Ms. Tailele at **www.JoanneTailele.com**

About the Illustrator

Joe Eckstein is the illustrator of over twenty-five books for children, including *Herby Gets a Life*, which he also authored. Drawing and writing stories since he can remember, he grew up in central Ohio, holds a Bachelor's degree in Fine Art, and has worked as a staff illustrator for a leading children's educational publisher. He has also taught art and theatre to children from kindergarten through eighth grade. Joe lives in Florida and is devoted to the wife of his youth, Kristen. When not creating art, he enjoys singing, performing in local theatre productions, traveling, being outdoors, and spending time with family. Learn more about Joe and his work at his web site, **www.JoeEckstein.com**.

Watch for more of

Carly's Island Adventures

at

www.JoanneTailele.com

CPSIA information can be obtained
at www.ICGtesting.com
Printed in the USA
BVHW022251170522
637228BV00002B/40